I0591723

Better Bones

Stories by

Jane-Rebecca Cannarella

Better Bones

ISBN: 978-0-578-22311-7

First Edition: August 2019

Cover design by Alexander Breth

Author photo by Cassandra Panek Photography

Product of the U.S.A.

For more titles and inquiries, please visit:

www.thirtywestph.com

Dedicated to the trips back and forth from Philadelphia to California which helped to define me, and to my cats: Easy Mac, Dream Phone, and Trash Cat.

TABLE OF CONTENTS

Better Bones

Couches I Knew in My 20s

In the dream I was having, I kept calling you John, even though that's not your name. It's the inverse of my name.

I met your ex-girlfriend on a couch owned by the boys I knew in my 20s and told her that you deserved your dog back. She liked me and I liked her, and we lay down on the couch and made out. She had tattoos on her thighs just like me, heat rash raising the ink lines just like on mine.

You walked in and got angry, but I couldn't figure out why—you get the dog back, and I like your ex-girlfriend.

After You Survive the Fallout—Shed

After it's over, shed. Shed your clothing—pull pieces of shirts and skirts and panties from your body like a snake escaping its skin. The debris from the fallout, raining acidy hurt from the heavens, coats your body: a nuclear exoskeleton; you are covered with the war. In the shower, hot water weeping over your pinked skin, slough off the outer layer of flesh. It still carries cells that hold the fingerprints of a person who once touched you. Clean yourself up like a cat with a forked tongue, sketching out memories and touches and handlings. The purple sheen on the curve of your ass marks the erasing of every smack you received, by request or uninvited.

Your body is a naked mole-rat, unseeing and tender. In each unpeeled layer, the imprints from embraces are released with each dying and dead cell. The sheet of skin at your feet looks like mildew while it slithers toward the drain. The fever of water surrounds you. Goodbye.

But even after the shower, radioactive material is still stuffed in your ears, holding every vibrating vocal reed from the people you wished were strangers. The shock wave has passed, but you carry every hurtful note of audible pulses: a voice crackling with Camel Blue cigarettes. Set a flame to Q-tips and singe the memories that come with that voice. Stir the seashell of your ear with the scorched cotton swab to free the echo. It's the same echoing voice that once, while sitting on blue plastic chairs at the Planned Parenthood watching *Step Up* and waiting to get your abortion, asked you, "Do you want to make out in the bathroom?" Get. Fucking. Gone.

Fission particles still lay among the threads of your hair. They are wounded soldiers who were propelled into the atmosphere and then descended onto and into you. Dust and ash are implanted, sown into your tresses like malignant crops. Shave it off. Or better still, rip it from the root like weeds—like corn silk gone rotten—and once they've been harvested, the strands lay at your toes. Wipe them away in waves.

When the rain-darkened soot has subsided, and the airburst is a memory—shed. Huddle in a ball with the boiling sea escaping from your eyes; fill up the atmosphere with everything that needs to be discarded.

Lose the past as the fruit of the sun melts from the sky, the lemon of your chest stinging with misery, bile climbing up your throat like a vine. Eliminate all the pieces that were infected by a disconnected orbit who crashed into you. The wreckage is upon you now, so destroy the rubble—the detritus doesn't own you anymore. Like a reptile, slough off the memories: the skin, the hair, the hearing, the parts of your body that are tied to the aftermath. Molted and unaided, in a ball with the ocean of the discarded, wait for the hurt of the fall to pass as it's replaced by what grows underneath.

Cartographer

When I turned grown-up, my body became a map: fault lines at the creases of my thighs; dots glowing in clusters at my shoulders, turning into constellations driving sailors home. Gin in my mouth became juniper in my blood—the kind of juice that staves off diseases.

As my covering shifted, I retreated into my frame—a silent ghost haunting the architecture of my interior. Every organ a cave, secreting myself in the middle-earth layers. I ran into rooms that locked from the inside.

Outside, an unruly formation has been crafted by quakes and tectonic plates shifting. If scientists looked closely, they could study my geology from the dry crust of hide to the sallow sinking meat.

My soil is pressed with indentations: imprints left by a trail of bodies—pilgrims who abandoned their journey while I was weighed down to the bed like a butterfly pinned and mounted under glass.

When I turned grown-up, there was still dew in my hair—a thicket resembling the Indiana Limberlost.

But branches of veins formed a new cratered desert on what was once a "me" that I finger-traced, a "me" that I knew so well. Entire pieces of my body divided into yellowing fragments, from uncharted ruins to unnavigable shapes crafted by the bends in my build.

My stomach is now full of pebbles, like a dinosaur swallowing rocks to help digest plants; the stones rattle with movement and I sound like a castanet. In younger years, I smiled so hard that it cracked my mouth full of crooked teeth. These hard smiles fashioned precious fractures in the incisors, and now my teeth have begun to resemble the prehistoric rubble that spots the water of my own Long Island Sound.

On one occasion, the Sound broke free and fell out of my eyes. The water gone, I dried my face and made it age. Salt left me a trailed corn husk and ripped my cheeks. When the skin opened and spilled, it turned into ash. Where once there were waterfalls, now ghost-white gunpowder lives: my face—the Wild West.

I matured into a lonely continent. My body, a friendless fuckless landmass, holds the history of looting pioneers. From the inside, I study and restudy the map of myself, a fossil boasting rocks like music, filled up and up with dinosaur stones.

Red Oxide of Iron

I thought about naming the freckles that spot your skin, nose to neck to shoulder. Spots on the back of your hands that I bend my neck down to examine individually: huddles of cinnamon constellations.

At one point eight years ago, I bought someone a stuffed animal that came with a star that you could name. I don't think he ever named the star—or the stuffed animal—and if he did, how would he ever find it in the phantasmagoria of the evening's complex patterns? So, I abandoned Outer Space. And I started naming patterns on people. Arrangements on your epidermis that mirror the Solar System. Complexions that parallel the Great Attractor.

I have fingerprint black and blues on the soft meat of my inner thighs from the whorls of your fingers. During the day, I vacation to the front of a mirror and press them, the tiny shocks of hurt reminding me of your dotted hands. I think about the loops and patterns and meanings of your fingertips. The Pleiades located at the end of your forearm. The dusting of freckles on your nose resting on my knees—a thousand superclusters.

There's a chocolate bar in my purse that you bought me. I rip ragged hunks off it, dirtying my fingernails—filled with the melting body of the candy as I paw at pieces. I hold it between my tongue and teeth. It seeps through the slack of my jaw, pooling against my soft and hard palate. The slice cut on my bottom lip burns when I tuck it between my central incisors. When I tip my chin toward the sky, the sweetness slips down my throat.

What's real that I can grasp in my fist? When you yield to the Hesperides, is it possible to account for the gravitational pull? Can you see the other side of the galaxy?

When my body's stopped orbiting, I touch the tip of my kingfisher-tongue to each pinpoint on you: beryllium, carbon, helium, iron.

Family of Four Lokos

Stephanie, John, and Hector spent an evening in early July selling their art on a sidewalk in Old City. The money—all pooled together—was enough to buy plenty of Four Lokos. They were the original recipe Four Lokos, filled with caffeine and famous for Jonestown-like massacres across college campuses. Stephanie knew about Four Loko and Joose way before frats did, staples of the diet of her former friends in Hazelton. In the heat of the cramped kitchen, the three drank the lot of it, unending cans into slack mouths with the occasional stream of neon green dribbling from the corners of their lips. It looked like the seepage from the 1991 movie *Teenage Mutant Ninja Turtles II: The Secret of the Ooze*, and for that, I always kind of liked it.

By the time I found the trio in the kitchen, they were prostrate across the ground rolling back and forth and eerily sing-songing, "Family. Family." John held a camcorder above his head and sang into the lens. Hector stubbed out his cigarettes into the linoleum, leaving little plastic craters in the floor. Dirt was tracked and ground into the kitchen floor so much that it became one with the tiles.

Like imploring children, they begged me to join in. "Janie, hi! Janie, hi! Play with us!" Stephanie, still on the floor, raised a can to me, and I took it from her elfish hand.

***

Several hours later, having endeavored to catch up, I sat on the floor in a sequined romper, unzipped to the waist because I had gained too much weight to force it into fitting. At some point, I thought it would be festive to dress up.

On one of my feet was an orange cheetah-patterned high heel—part of a pair that Catherine bought me—the other heel kicked off and across the room. When I was a little kid there was a line of stuffed animals—kitty cats and jungle cats and other various members of the genus Acinonyx—where the head of the plushy was filled with marbles. When you cuddled it, the marbles would purr. The abandoned high heel, wounded and propped against a ceramic statue of a fisherman holding a lantern, looked like the cheetah version of those stuffed animals.

I smoked Pall Mall Blues and half crouched over a 40 of Coors. Next, to me, Stephanie hoovered deli meat down her gullet. She was the type of girl that said she was vegetarian but ate meat. And, like, a lot of it. She spread round slices of beige turkey in a line and ate them in a row off the floor.

The malt liquor tasted like the candy that I used to spend every saved cent on at the snack shack at the community pool seventeen years earlier. I mixed beer, gin, soda with whiskey—in between sips of the lime-colored pint—the booze was a Gobstopper of inebriants. In 6th grade, my best friend Emily took me to her family's fancy golf club. I asked how much the chewy Spree cost and she said it was free. "Free" in the sense that, in our youth, we didn't know what a charge to an account meant. I ate sleeve after sleeve of chewy Spree until my stomach ached. Feeling disgusting in the humidity, too sick to jump into the pool at the club, I became a puddle in the heat. Abstentious Emily, the product of a weight loss-obsessed mother, made an impossible height on the diving board and slipped under the water. I watched her jackknife dives while holding my extended stomach.

***

Hector vomited Four Loko on my thighs and then rested an exhausted head against my shoulder. I didn't move him. The puke was a warm embrace. It seeped into my panties. It filled the craters on the floor from the cigarettes. I rested my head on top of his; Stephanie and John were already asleep in the recovery position near the oven.

***

Mark returned from his second shift job and towered over us—a Converse-wearing Cronos. Our bodies blocked the refrigerator door; he couldn't get to his dinner. He wouldn't be able to drink his beers since those were consumed earlier in the evening—after the dress-up but before the deli meat.

He placed paper towels that stuck like a second skin on my thighs. He pulled Hector's hair off his cheeks, stuck in clumps to the drying puke on his face. While rolling John on his side, Stephanie woke up to drowsily sing-song: "Family. Family."

The Origin of Trees

Palm trees belong to two states: California and Florida. But more to California than Florida—Florida is where oranges grow on trees that are the result of shoots sprouting out of the state's belly button. Palm trees are from coughs in the soil—rumbling in-your-chest coughs that leave the state with swells that looks like the pokey veins in my mom's hands.

Palms wander like aliens in the American South: creeping interlopers hiding against shingled houses; strangers in the swamp, growing and stretching fronds like bat wings. I prefer them in the desert where they cast shade and house the rats that my terrier would kill in groups to leave as gifts for my dad.

In Philadelphia, there are no palm trees. There are trees that die and resurrect, like prickly Christs. And trees that smell like sex during the spring. And an Osage orange tree on Ridge Avenue with its bizarre fruit in the summer. And trees near Clark Park where urban foragers gather its berries, but I don't know its name.

During a summertime trip to a house on the New Jersey shore, Angela brought paper bags filled with groceries. She baked cactus paddles and spread honey and goat cheese on top. I held the oar of the cactus against my tongue, the fibers of a used-to-be home in my mouth—not quite a palm tree, but foliage I was familiar with, nonetheless. My acid mouth turned the cactus into a green paste, and the pulp slid down my throat like tears.

I don't know the name of any summertime trees that live on the East Coast.

Wintertime in Philadelphia, the sky bleeds white and erases the landscape. The city is monochrome, and the naked trees share the richness of their silent language with one another. Philadelphia becomes a Xerox of a Xeroxed version of itself, the landscape barely visible during hushing snowstorms. Treebones blot the quieting sky until only the edges of the city remain.

Outside of a house in West Philadelphia, a tree grew from only one wild seed bred by John Bartram. Later his son William would name the tree Franklinia in honor of his dad's good friend Dr. Ben Franklin. Perhaps the largest Franklinia in the world, the tree died during a snowstorm the first year I moved to the city. I still look at its bleached remains from my apartment across the street, its open body a detailed record of its palm-tree-less environment.

Ocean Songs for the Nursery

Josh once told me that he liked the ocean because, when he went under a wave, it reminded him that life doesn't go on forever. The cradle of his body rocked to hush-a-bye inches from the seabed. Life momentarily stilled while the smaller seas played a lillibullero. I liked the ocean, too.

In the years that followed the sea singing Josh its lullaby, I ended up very far from the ocean.

In a moment of quiet, I replicate Josh by sinking underneath the water in a claw tooth bathtub—a key feature of crumbling row homes throughout all parts of Philadelphia. The sides of the tub sheathed in peeling lead paint and sheets of mildew; tiles filled with grout that resembles the slime and slickness of seaweed I dreaded getting on my skin or in my hair. Years prior, back home in the saltwater, I once stepped on a shelf of mossy rocks, and the ocean fuzz got under my toenails. At rest in the waters of the bath, I worry that the black moss of the tub will catch underneath my fingernails as I grip its sill, steadying myself in a straight line during the under-tap-water reprieve.

I open my eyes under the water, and they sting like they would if opened under saltwater, my hair a witch's tangle around my shoulders. I wonder if this is what the world of death would feel like. Holding my breath and intermittently streaming bubbles in angry bursts, I shift my weight to make swells. I am my own wake.

Disturbing the underwater by shimmying my thighs together, the water laps and ripples and distorts the surface of a wish-to-be ocean. The cradlesong of the sea means that a person can take solace knowing that life isn't an eternity. But I don't know if bathtub waves sing the same song.

Detritus from the dirty tub sticks in my arm hair—garbage rockfish that live in the foresty kelp of the body. I run out of breath listening to the blood in my ears, the same swirling sound of conch shells. But I don't hear the relief that's found in nursery rhymes in the indentations of salty waves. Deserting the tub, I bring breakers of the bath-ocean with me. Kneeling in observation next to the filmy porcelain, there are flakes of paint that have fallen into the tub— flotsam on man-made combers. Bending over the bath, I make my own miniature waves, using the energy of breath and blowing across the surface of the waters.

I might not know the release that comes with the ocean's soothing songs, but I'll find a way to get under the waves, find majesty in the uncertainty of the surf, exist in the gap between the ocean and the sun where life doesn't go on forever.

Pendulum Pastry

I saw a woman outside the grocery store, Supremo, on 43rd. Bowed hips cocked in the way I really like, puffer jacket open exposing bits of feather stuffing, a smooth navel soft with downy hair rigged into sloping sextant hip points. She navigated her stance into an arch.

She unwrapped a pie—the fragile body of the pastry in a flimsy tin—and proceeded to bend the disposable pan in half, dipped one hand into the pie, and pulled out chunks with a bear fist—fervor mouth filled with fruit.

***

I remember that boys in middle school had mouths that tasted like things: the boy with the cherry lifesaver cheeks, the one with milk breath—taking kisses from one another in the closet at the back of the classroom, flipping quarters to see which boy kissed which girl.

Eighth grade was a fucking mess with all the cool boys carrying Binaca—they never played quarters to see who kissed who. The fly kids positioned themselves using time, genes, directions, and speed—dead reckoning—to ensure that their mint mouths fed off one another.

I hate aerosol mint and the boys that are now men who tasted like it.

***

The woman outside Supremo, time, and space, body slightly over the garbage near the electronic door, made a mess of the pie in what seemed like a second. Before I could even cross the street, the flakes were shaken into her jaw. Spiny fingers in the tin fishing out the last bits of sweet fruit, dough, wet insides. Once the pie was devoured—pendulum pastry balanced in time—her hands crushed the pan, striking down with ferocious intensity, digits dyed red with berries looking like shrapnel over Christmas lights.

The woman spiked the exoskeleton pan into the trash—all one smooth movement. It thudded while she left. One second she was there, the next she was a shadow against the horizon with hair pouring behind her like the whipping sail of a full-rigged ship.

What inspired her hunger, the intensity and ruthlessness, and wildness and savagery when faced with this dessert? I wonder what merciless mouths taste like—are they the strawberry-shaped lips of sailing ship women with feather-down bodies, or are they the bitter nip of kisses carried in cans?

When I got to the garbage can outside the electronic door, I looked at the shattered remains of the tin body—mouth agape in deathly moratorium, crimson insides slick in the corners. Only the gentle skin of the crust shed in snowflake sizes near the damp body remained.

The door slid open with my hovering, unfastening hinges to the dazzlingly bright insides of Supremo: a beacon, a compass—the table closest to the door covered in sweets.

A Thicket. A Glen.

We were trying to figure out what a deer's home is called. A thicket? A glen? A clearing?

The train rocked and I fell into you, and the warmth of your hand righting me brushed my thigh, and the spot burned. I bit my lip thinking about you touching me, and I hoped you'd notice, but we kept talking about deer until the landscape changed into the city.

I got off at my spot to go to someone's home that wasn't yours, and you went home to who-knows-what, but it wasn't me.

The sound of a different person's voice irritated me out of the fog of thinking about you and deer and the place on my leg where your fingers landed. While he talked, I painted your face on him—a medley of your features—until he became a disjointed Picasso fragmentation. He was an imaginary You puppet—part himself, but mostly someone else. While he stayed a moving simulacrum, I nodded and nodded and thought about the rhythm of the train.

Later that night, kept awake by the sound of a stranger's breathing, I thought about you and deer and if tomorrow the train would jostle me into your path again.

Shrimp Backs

J likes it when I spit in his mouth during sex. He says it makes him feel dirty in a way that turns him on.

It's not hard for me to be dirty. I have a small angry scratch on my neck that I worry is infected because the collar of my dress is grubby. It's a jagged rectangle on my nape that I pester with my fingertips before removing the thin cotton shift. Standing in a musty room, the dappled sunlight bounces off the smudged windows and makes shadow puppets on our bodies. J's hips are patterned in stretch marks. They look like the tracks in old porcelain bathtubs.

Years earlier, I once told a different boy—so many of them in a line, at the same time, at conjoining times—that if I ever quit drinking, taking baths would be my higher power. I would thaw in hot water surrounded by oily bubbles in our crumbling apartment while he cooked spaghetti in the kitchen. Our small world turned foggy with the steam.

I told that same different boy from years earlier, after spats about wasting water, that I was thinking about getting dry shampoo. I waved the spray can under his nose while shopping at the CVS on 40th Street. His blue eyes crossed with the motion and he said, "I don't think you need to start taking dust baths like a chinchilla."

Now I take to the bathtub while I drink. I sit in the water and sink underneath the scummy pool—the top of the water a sheen from the unwashed tub. I get my hair wet because if my hair is wet, I'm clean...maybe.

The dry shampoo was never purchased. And there is no longer steam from spaghetti in the adjoining room. I rest in the bathtub with the droplets falling off my body. I let my bathtub-hair air dry. It dries in greasy mats.

My body lives in the dirty. Like a heat-seeking missile, it negotiates itself onto other bodies, detonating in agonizing bursts. I find other people that are dirty, or want to be dirty or are just lonely, and our neediness is filth that makes us feel less alone whether we're washed or unwashed.

I find J. We undress, and there is dust in the filigree of his body hair. I spit in his mouth, and the cut on my neck is a vase for our sweat.

We're both stinking animals.

The dirt under my fingernails resembles the slim lines of a shrimp's back before they're deveined. Is that line of blackness the sea bug's waste? I eat shrimp with their filth intact because I'm too lazy to care, the same as how I chew on my nails to clean and cut them. I only ever trouble the blotches from under my fingertips when the thought of strangers seeing the grime embarrasses me. If I was still little, my mom would make me scrub my nails with the pink Barbie toiletry set, even though the soft-bristled nail brush never truly got the job done. I preferred lathering with the Barbie shower glove, moving my velvet hand over the curve of my belly. Nail brushes never impressed me.

My black shrimp-back nails vacation in the quicksand of J's skin; they sink into the muscle and make me think of crustaceans perched on the floor of the ocean. My fingers are antennae tasting him. Colonies of hands, back and forth, seek to know foreign bodies. Underwater figures feed on the masses and liquid of one another. How well does a shrimp know the ocean?

I don't care where I've gotten the crust underneath my fingernails—subways, sponges, laundry filters. When I'm anxious, my fingers either go into my mouth or into the meat of boys' backs—dirt transferred from body to sea, like how the spit transfers from me to J. I never get sick, no matter how dirty the ocean becomes.

My Favorite Recipe for *Eraserhead* Pizza

This guy and I fucked on a couch in my first apartment while *Eraserhead* played in the background, an early June sunset turning the shitty basement squalor into the color of a cleft peach. And since then, I've never been able to watch the movie the whole way through without getting wet—a Pavlovian response to memories of grabby hands roughly cupping my tits, calloused fingers fumbling with the cotton of my good-girl panties. Not that a young Jack Nance couldn't get it, too.

We ordered pizza after having sex and sat naked on the couch under a maroon airline blanket. In movies about adults, I noticed the adult apartments always had a throw blanket over the back of the sofa, so the airline blanket—perfect for post-coital modesty—lived on top of the blue couch that was stolen from my old college campus. We got Pizza Hut; I had spent a lifetime making up for missed Pizza Hut parties by way of large stuffed-crust pizzas with two toppings of pepperoni.

Waiting for the pizza, we watched the Beautiful Girl Across the Hall do her hot girl thing; Jack Nance's character looked to score. The guy made a couple of remarks about her while I shifted my weight from side to side, letting the cushions absorb the sogginess from my thighs. Supposedly David Lynch was influenced by his experiences in a bad neighborhood in Philly—coincidental because the guy and I were watching the movie in our own troubled Philly neighborhood. The apartment buzzer rang during the scene where Nance was having visions, and I, dressed in his boxers and a winter coat I found crumpled next to the couch, got the pizza. When I brought the pizza back, I awkwardly got naked as to not leave the guy alone in his nudity under the sheet.

We ate pieces of pepperoni and crusts filled with cheese while Nance butchered the monster baby's organs with scissors. The thick liquid that covered the deformed child sort of looked like the cheesy crust and the mess of fluids and non-Newtonian-like substances from real life and *Eraserhead* life made me feel gross and swampy.

The guy stroked my hair with greasy fingertips, getting tangled in the rat's nest of curls—the result of sex hair and unremarkable hygiene. Nance was awash in a mushroom cloud of eraser shavings on screen, his image occasionally shimmering due to a blemish on the VHS tape.

White light and white noise filled the television as the movie ended. We let the din swallow us— unsettling noises intended to unsettle—and I dropped my head on his shoulder. The grease had seeped into the pizza box and made Rorschach shapes while the credits rolled.

Having missed most of the movie the first time, we agreed to rewind it and start the whole thing again, holding the rewind button down the entire time. We watched the film run backward: planet un-erupting, monster baby's organs jumping back into its swaddling, blood un-oozing, sex with the Girl Across the Hall un-encountered.

If there was a way I could swap orgasms for just one *Fern Gully* Pizza Hut party, I would.

Cards on the Floor in the Shape of a T

For a short time, I lived with three witchy women—an eye-roll-inducing name that they called themselves. The trio were smoky girls who painted coal eyeliner on their waterline and left rings of red lipstick on the edges of clove cigarettes. They didn't wear ill-fitting peasant tops; they weren't obsessed with fantasy novels. All three luxuriated around the apartment like bored cats, hanging off the arms of couches. Each draped herself over a favorite piece of shitty, secondhand furniture.

My witches were named after Greek prophets and songs from the '70s. Our place was filled with pestles and mortars and handmade tapestries and burning herbs and rocks they called crystals. One time I threw away a cracked piece of amber glass and experienced their fury for destroying a tiger's eye. It looked like a piece of sharp garbage.

During humid evenings, our resident prophet of doom would divine the future by placing cards on the floor in the shape of a T. She'd wave the painted figures in front of our faces, proclaiming the power of the eight of swords. The poet crone told me about the fantastic sex that was in my future after looking at the dredges of tea leaves in my mug. A prayer for the future, I spun the cup on top of the saucer three times with my left hand.

The witchy women would vacillate between mysticism and the mundane every day, existing somewhere in the purgatory of reality.

I'd come home to a note on the door that said:

ᛒᚢᛘ ᛏᚨᛘᛈᚠᛏᛋ

which means "buy tampons" in ancient runic symbols.

Before they went to sleep, the girls would gather like a nest of field mice in a large bed with a black comforter. They watched reality TV shows and drank Malibu rum, and in the morning our lake goddess' painted-on eyebrows would be clouded smudges.

On the back of my astrological birth chart, one of them had written an angry note about the dishes not being done. Scrawled underneath was a second note explaining how we needed to break our old broom and leave the pieces at a previous apartment because we'd obviously brought the past's bad energy with us.

I'd come home to the witches crowded on a couch, dipping their hands into a paper bucket of fried chicken—their cauldron of power. 00Heads on each other's shoulders, they watched reruns of *Gilmore Girls*. Someone had just burnt green garden sage in the apartment. Our home smelled like Thanksgiving.

The Practice of Eating Apples with Glass Teeth

There isn't a bathroom in Philadelphia that I haven't thrown up in—from the tattered mirrored black-and-white-checked tiles of Kung Fu Necktie with the ground dappled in either spit or semen, to the stalls of Johnny Brenda's with couples kissing near that weirdly opulent goldish couch, to the elegance of the powder room at the Rittenhouse Hotel. My job. The Ritz Bourse. That time I ended up at a Chili's in Center City on New Year's Eve, 2013.

I long for the coziness of spearing my tenderly marred fingers across my slug-tongue, oily bubbles of anxiety bursting and erupting through my esophagus, past my now-gravely larynx, and covering my chipped teeth, spilling onto the toilet and the floor. Or in the case of my home on 42nd and Chestnut, clogging the white porcelain sink and the black mildewed tub.

If cumming is a release, puking is physiotherapy. And I'm pretty sure I don't binge or purge or diet or food-obsess. Never. Not really. I surf the frenzy of worry and the chemical urgency of flight and fight by resting my head against the putrid cool plastic seat and wait for the shaking racks of my stomach.

Sometimes the two-pointed fingers feel like cranky accusations, and my body likes to refute the debate of my judgmental hands.

I've learned to say "delicious" in four different languages, and I try to pierce apple flesh with my incisors but always avoid using my tree stump molars.

I hang out in front of the toothpaste-spattered mirror in my bathroom and look at the cellophane teeth, at how they become opaque when I push my tongue against them.

Elegy for a Blue Crab

How does the crab define himself? Where does he feel most alive? For a critter that lives in all the waters and sometimes the land and occasionally the sky, what is the defining trait for high-tempered nippers?

From 100 to 700 AD, the Moche civilization admired the crab and depicted the sidestepping crustacean in their pottery, later becoming russet-colored shards of clay in the hands of land-dwelling archeologists. The ancient Andeans probably saw the shuffle of a wandering ghost crab in the sands near their part of Peru, sacred in its locomotion as it made its way back to the sea.

Like the waning cycles of the moon, the crab casts off his shell and exists between the balance of the living and dead: rock pets with personality.

In Moche ceramics, over 500 pieces are sexual in nature—along with the crab art. A number of the pieces depict skeletons being masturbated by living women, cages of bones contorted with the agony of carnality. Some scholars believe that the Moche art served as a teaching model to show the relationship between the now and the hereafter. What kind of sex do the crabs have in Moche ceramics? Do their exoskeleton prisons shake with voluptuous gratification, too? What did the crustaceans teach civilization of life and the afterlife?

***

Russell is from Maryland, so he knows a lot about crabs, and he likes to talk about the Chesapeake and all that lived there. He said that in the Chesapeake Bay there is so much fishing line that it's unsafe for deep-water divers because they can't see more than a couple of inches in front of their faces. The bay's basement is a murderous quilt of nylon thread.

Russell told me that at one point, before the fishing line, there were so many crabs in the Chesapeake that they would crawl, of their own volition, into woven baskets dropped into the water. This image makes me think of bare legs in flowing water with crabs slowly climbing those bodies until the crustacean arrives willingly to the person's lips.

Where did the crabs go when their homes became wire?

***

According to Russell, the best part of the crab is called "crab fat," and I like the idea of the stone bodies having an internal fattiness that's a secret until you crack open the orange shell. But when I research crab fat, I find that it's just the guts of the crab and not fatty parts at all. There is no porterhouse part of a crustacean.

As it turns out "crab fat" is the same thing as "crab butter" and "crab mustard." I would have never thought that the viscera and roe of the piercers could be so versatile. The actual word is *tomalley* and it should only be consumed in small quantities because it contains so many toxins and PCBs. Just like with real dairy butter—small yet meaningful quantities only.

PCB is a pollutant that moves up the food chain, and in some instances, it's known to cause cancer. So, the constellation, while it's on Earth, is potentially a carrier for its namesake.

***

The mustard of a Maryland blue crab is less the color of yellow mustard at baseball games and more like spicy brown mustard on expensive deli sandwiches. When I tell Russell about the PCBs, he is immediately concerned that he's dying of cancer.

I really want his astrological sign to be Cancer—a human crab that talks about crabs that contain a disease that shares the name of the crab's constellation. If Russell was one of the admired crustaceans of the Moche people, his main concerns would be combat or copulation, which isn't too unlike his personality.

But he's not a crab. He's a goat.

***

As a little kid, I always wanted a pet, but despite my vocal fussiness my parents never relented. Since breathing pets didn't present themselves as an option, I decided to collect the bodies of dead crabs from the shoreline of Long Island Sound. In my red plastic sand bucket, I'd gather the limp figures of crustacea to take home as my in-between-life friends.

I'd confide in their stone forms and named each after favorite cartoon characters (Jem, Scooby, Lion-o). In their death, the beautiful swimmers with the fractures in their shells would make the entire house smell like low tide. Crabs on the shelf, our home lived in the ocean. But while I slept, my parents would throw out my hollow friends. In the morning I was convinced that they had returned to the ocean.

I assumed that the crabs necromanced themselves back to life, and I'd stand in the shallows with my feet gripping the mossy rocks underneath, looking for my companions. Schools of minnows would tap my stomach while I searched the water. Sometimes a stray thread of fishing line would float by.

I was disappointed that my crab friends never returned. They became pale specters in memories of loneliness—childhood ghost crabs—but not the same as the ghost crabs the Moche once knew.

***

Only recently did I learn that the crabs I collected and mourned were blue crabs: the Maryland state crustacean—the very type of crab that Russell's body was raised on. The tides of the Atlantic brought the bodies to both of us, though our intentions toward them were totally different.

Eventually, we would become adults with passionate and compassionate feelings about crabs, and constellations, and constellations of crabs. Sometimes I imagine us as children—him spreading the butter of blue crabs on pieces of bread, me talking to the vacant shells of seagull-consumed buddies.

How does the crab define himself? I think of my phantom former ocean friends—ancient, revered, tweezing mystics—using their sidling magic to close the distance between the Chesapeake and the Sound. They are spirits in shells that span time, twisting invisible fishing wire that entangles the two of us together.

The Shape of Rain

The warehouse where the muddle-artists live has an indoor treehouse. It's there that I'm split kneed, balanced with my hands in fists against a red pipe, hiding money in a lockbox above a bed that I sometimes share with a boy covered in freckles. I look at a triangular corner of the ceiling where yellow insulation peeks out and think about how it could house a family of birds, what nests could be made in the indents of ceilings—little homes created from brittle sheets of padding for lost, hollow-boned beauties.

Later in the evening, the skies spit weather. When it rains, the treehouse erupts with the sound of quarters bouncing off the beams. As a pair, the freckled boy and I are on our backs, looking up, trying to see the sound. The warehouse shakes itself alive under the dropping water, and I squeeze my eyes tight untill little explosions of white appear beneath the lids, bursts of colorless fireworks. I focus on the whiteness and the washing machine sounds of the sky. It makes me think of how hollow rain sounded when I was younger.

In the basements of my twenties, the rain made shushing sounds while droplets sputtered in through the many broken windows. With tenements crumbling, you become used to broken windows—the norm when you're the tenant of slumlords. Like a stammering watering can, the grey clouds and jagged glass openings of forgotten windows fed viney weeds that grew in the humidity of the kitchen. The kitchen weeds marked the sallow passage of time—a clock made of leafy climbers working their way into a fading home.

When the basement jungle closed its doors to me due to lack of money, I became a papier-mâché bird that found homes in crevices that only existed in discolored spaces. Shapeless and directionless, I created nests in disappearing terrains occupied by fellow wanderlusting acquaintances. I made space for myself in the cracks of cushions on shitty trash-picked sofas owned by boys whose names I would eventually forget.

***

The current version of me doesn't want to think about those couches or the parade of boys from my twenties, so instead, I press my crushed-fruit mouth against a blur of freckles to pull myself into the moment, to find a way to be present, in the now. I let body weight and dewdrops of sweat feed my pores, falling precipitation that sustains my molted skin like a plant. Pressing my face against the boy's damp neck, I pull the taste of wet skin salt into the corner of my mouth. I store the sip against chipped teeth so I can drink from it later.

My sister once dated a boy that has the same name as the boy that I'm in love with—the one who lives in a tree in a warehouse, with the freckles in a semi-circle on his eyelids. I want to ask my sister if something about the shared names is meaningful. But I don't, because that boy existed during the days of her own basement youth and, like mine, those days ended. For the moment, I want to be grounded in a space where there are no endings. So, I irritate the pulp of my mouth, trace a fingertip over the cloud of eye freckles, curl my fists into his damp flesh before touching the walls of the treehouse. Before falling asleep, I stretch to the full length of my hollow bones.

The Binding Sequence

During the summer of the thrift store eyelet dress, I scraped my chin while drunk on whatever I found in the cabinet. I told my best friend that everyone should live their lives like they were stuck in the opening of a teen television drama. My hands, vigilant and un-resting, crawled through clots of soapy water washing away earth and gluiness and the smell of sweat.

I violently flew on swing sets, babbling lyrics to songs I've now forgotten, breath stained with whiskey. My hands were always seemingly clammy with grime since it was the season of sex in the park in the middle of the night—different times with different people, in a corner of the playground near a miniature bridge that crossed a dried-up stream.

I embraced the role of a disgraceful young woman if there really is such a thing. And if so, I was honored to be the part. Dirty hair with clumps of mud planted in between the tendrils, the knots from motion bundled on the back of my head.

And very shortly later on, there was the time the homeless guy sitting on a stoop in Center City told the boy I was in love with "She isn't even beautiful, man" while we ambled past. He said, "That's not nice" in return, which just made me feel worse. I wore the dress that had the dirt stains at the apex of the wings of my shoulder blades. When I craned my neck down and touched the tips of my shoulders, I felt like I might be able to fly.

The heat drove people to unprecedented candor that year. This was around the same era that I pinched the skinny flesh around my humerus, the preoccupation with being infatuated acting as my food. The short-lived inspiration and admiration bloomed in my stomach where my favorite snacks used to live. I ate starvation because I couldn't digest anything but my many romantic fixations.

The suburbs became an island where people couldn't escape. I tried to pluck out mournful melodies on toy instruments, points, and counterpoints in a tinny fugue that eventually became aural memories of shadowy figures who ceased to care after a while.

A man that I realized a decade later was still a boy once told me that my meanness was disgusting, so I jumped out of his idling car into a night where the damp humidity melted into my exposed limbs. I shouted "Fuck" at his car, not even bothering to finish the sentiment. I wondered how far I could push people into breaking—if that was a power that anyone actually had.

In future years, with additional ounces that matched the passing of time, no one would hunt for me, so I'd grab fistfuls of my own flesh to remember what it felt like when lost girls were wanted.

Bison Called Buffalo

"One of the top five kisses of all time" made me cringe the most. Like you could quantify that. And then you tried to describe that time in the outdoor 1 AM when we fumblingly calculated punctuated-mouth-on-other-mouth. Startled by ever-persistent stomach butterflies, we still tried to impress each other but ended up frightening and becoming frightened by a passing doe. Though we were acting out a cliché, the pureness of our feelings seemed to erase the embarrassment. At the time, it seemed sincere.

You ended up calling it love, but only years later.

How do two people argue about whether it's called a buffalo or a bison, marring moments where our teeth knocked each other? "There aren't any fucking buffaloes in the US. They were bison." Later, I twisted my ankle at your retreating back. I don't think we were arguing about quadrupeds.

Static years later, the internet told us we are perfect for one another. Which is a shame that it didn't tell us that after the kissing and the deer and the bison called buffalo.

In an airport in Denver, we swapped war stories over wavy lines and the squinting glare of crappy phones. I ate THC-laced chocolate and waited for a plane that was 12 hours away from liftoff. You kept me company while I dumped overpriced beer on top of legalized candy, sloshing in my stomach while the wings of insects beat against my ribs, again. You messaged encouragements when I got sick to my stomach and my eyes were all foggy. You said the cringe-worthy thing about kisses that happened before a lifetime of silence. It made me smile, but I might have been drunk.

I pressed the hot phone against my cheek while it buzzed message after message from you, and the sheen on my face made plocking sounds every time I pulled it away to read your thoughts.

I used to Google search our names with plus signs in between them because I liked to see us still linked together. And I reminded myself to dislike you, often to keep you alive. I placed pins in memories of grass blankets at 1 AM and does, and deer, and kissing. And how I used to know you. All so that on a pilled carpet in Colorado, the adult me could love the stranger of adult you.

Hypnotized with Motion

I didn't suck on any honeysuckle this year. And am reminded of this loss while looking at unremarkable green bushes with clusters of golden flowers that frame the side of the road during my commute. I didn't suck on any honeysuckle last year, either. Or the year before that. Or the decade before that. But as a kid, I would pull flower on top of flower off their bending branches, sticking the slim filament in my mouth, searching for the promised taste of honey—never quite getting it, but almost.

The cool kids would spend their summer money on fries and strawberry shortcake ice cream bars, while I'd chew on the inside of flora—the petals like damp tissue paper. I never had summer money. Flowers come cheap.

The year the lobsters disappeared for good—fished out of Long Island following decades of overfishing—the honeysuckle bush died. From that summer on, the Long Island Sound wouldn't feed families summer lobsters, cooking them alive in gigantic pots—my uncle describing the process, beer against his lips, as "making dead, that bug." I spent the summer of the lost lobsters and dead honeysuckle snapping at the small swollen leaf buds. I would scratch the branches with my fingernail, searching for a green indication of life, pawing at the twigs trying to find the wick of the branch. The bush was removed since dead bushes serve no purpose. They can't provide shade, or foliage, or flowers to feed adolescents.

As a teen, I chewed on sourgrass waiting for rides after school, the strange desert world of California didn't grow the honeysuckles of my younger youth. I stopped eating sourgrass after getting sick from the pesticide sprayed on them. I never thought of them as weeds until that point. From the balcony of my room, I could see eclipsed mountains bordering Mexico, the sun sinking behind them, casting ridged peaks into verses of solidity. I learned to quietly dance fingers up and down the slopes of not-yet-broad shoulders, the end-of-day orange in my eyes, the feeling of sun-warmed landscapes beneath my teeth, the taste of almost-honey-but-not on sunburned skin. From that point on, I feasted on new types of flesh.

Turning twenty, I was on the coast of a rock-filled beach somewhere in England, where waves are born grey and heavy. The surf was a stomach of unsure fluttering, tickled quaky movements with shards of light bouncing off the surf—a motion I'd seen before, mirrored in goose bumped navels. I lifted a smooth, round stone at the edge of the sea to my lips, rolled it in my mouth to taste the salt. The beaches of the lobster-less Long Island Sound were also filled with stones that I would place against my tongue.

A lifetime later, after a snowstorm in Colorado, I couldn't tell if the distance was water or land, and indefinite lengths were the blues of half-opened eyes measured in ice and vastness. Driving through the snow-filled state, I ate old Christmas ribbon candy to pass the time, spent mile marker amounts of time melting the sugar glass against my teeth, puking on the side of the road because I ate too much.

In Spain, there is an ancient restaurant where I pulled apart pieces of chicken, grease glossing my cheeks. The fragile bones in between my teeth like the bird wings of boys' backs I knew in my youth, during the times when honeysuckles fed me their almost-tastes. I rip apart the tiny body. Hands drenched. Consumed frenetically. Devoured with gusto. Hypnotized with motion.

The Scent of Frozen Flowers

When we got to the house with the lemon tree in California, I climbed up the thin branches and pulled down the fruit. I made a joke about Eve. We tossed the yellow ball back and forth, the sun dazzling our eyes every time we tried to land the catch.

Back in Philadelphia, in our kitchen filled with dead flowers, the empty pizza boxes are stacked up past the ledge of the window. The cat that we named Trash likes to sit atop the boxes and look out at a backyard that's filled with the wreckage from the apartment getting gutted next door.

When I toss out the mountain of pizza boxes, I frisbee one into the garbage and see it's from a pizza place that went out of business, back from a time that we were still happy.

I kept the lemon from the backyard of the California house. I press it to my face and hope that it will act as a time machine transporting us back to heat-filled early summer days when I was silent and contented. The lemon is going bad and is soft in my hand, no longer the hard ball that we tossed around. I think about eating it to keep a part of those days in me forever.

As I empty the kitchen of its garbage, I throw away the special water dish that I bought to keep my cat alive and drinking easily, but he's dead now anyway, and every time I look at it, the creeping emptiness that lives in the pit of my stomach grows. It spreads up and through my chest, spirals around my heart. I think of my heart as the kindergarten shape instead of an organ. The shape is where love lives; the organ is clinical and just keeps the blood pumping.

I imagine petting the empty blackness that crawls up my chest and lodges in my throat—bitter bile that reminds me of how the acid of lemonade would fill my mouth.

From the fridge, I throw away all the Tupperware I bought to help me lose weight: plastic dishes that portion control every calorie that I put in my body. I don't want orange lids and baby-food green containers controlling me anymore. I sit on the dirty and damp kitchen tiles and eat the last of the Easter chocolate I find in the freezer. It's July. The milk chocolate films my cheeks and clusters in the corners of my mouth like in the photos of me as a baby.

When I get to the dead flowers, I don't know whether or not to throw them out. One is a bouquet from a wedding we were both in—best man and bridesmaid. I caught the flowers cavalierly while drunk and brandished them over my head like a torch. We joked about the implications of catching the bundle of white roses, but before the conversation got too serious, we made jokes about how the white roses are a weird symbol for purity used during a symbolic occasion representing unity. Someone joked about how red roses, a symbol of passion, are probably never used for weddings because a future of togetherness doesn't seem that fiery. I don't remember which one of us made that crack. After the festivities ended, I left them to dry on the counter: a reminder of a potential tomorrow.

When the kitchen is emptied of all the garbage, only the rotten lemon and the frozen bouquet remain.

Plural Axes Play

Scott's voice is like a hollow boat. Only certain people have boat voices, and Scott's sounds like an empty hull. The ocean tends to be indifferent, and he's committed to reading aloud the fantasy novel that he wrote in high school—well over a decade earlier—while we lie in bed. I listen without stopping for over an hour. I think about the armor I've developed over the years to guard myself against future spells of silence that later wait.

I tally up people in my head, a nodding collection of the same faces, culled from the same garden—maybe numbering in the 30s? 40s? I think about the Einstein quote, the one about madness and repetitive behaviors. I'm mad—not mad angry, but maybe that too. I've lived this moment before, which for a brief second makes me feel immortal before it makes me feel empty. The repetition and immorality remind me of the family in my favorite children's book; their familiar eternal faces swim in front of my eyes. Still locked in my brain the way I imagined them, they live their same plot for the rest of days, wading through my memories to keep me company.

Restless and sullen, I tell faceless Scott and his hollow voice that he's what William Blake's line breaks would look like if they were human. I trace shapes on his bare skin. Do waves ever stop distorting?

When I was a little girl, I used to draw missing dog posters while my mom did schoolwork at the local library. I didn't have a dog—though prayed for one desperately—and I figured this would be the best way to get one. Asking went unnoticed, my liturgical entreaties remained unanswered, and the lonesomeness went up under lavender-colored magnets displayed on the fridge.

I do the same thing now with strange bodies. Making markers of my fingers, I sketch hopeful words on exposed limbs, my lips, larynx, and tongue ghost-still. I trust to perdition and let my body roll on lapping waves, my vision shadowed with the image of hundreds of lost dog illustrations floating atop my ocean of armor— Scott's voice still a boat in the air.

Freckles

The cinnamon freckles that are dusted on my body are identical to the ones on the bodies of my sometimes-former, sometimes-current, nighttime, kind-of friends (I wouldn't go as far as to call the speckled procession lovers). When our bodies combined, the specks could soak up twice the amount of vitamin D, especially in a dark room.

Ephelides awoke in the sunshine, but stormy weather would wash away the little stains, and the outer patch of my skin would become weary during overcast days. Once the summertime came, I would seek out other individual freckles, looking for myself in the soil of other people's skin.

Human freckles often yielded varying results.

***

James and I once matched the freckles on our shoulders while sitting on a bed-bugged mattress in South Philly. We compared the variants in the patterns of our brown splotches, his less dark and less visible. They looked like shadowed designs in old lace curtains.

Our spots were little twin blueprints that we touched together, matching each other's skin on a mattress dotted with the black blood from vampire pests.

So many tessellations in one room.

In the morning, his freckled arm bumped up against my freckled arm. A maroon spot was alive on his bicep, and it crawled from him on to me. Its flat body decided to lie on top of a mole on my forearm, distinctly not an ephelis.

I left that morning. I never went back.

***

But not every textured stranger stayed a brief splotchy visitor. And sometimes I could see the shapes of what I was pursuing in the silhouettes of a scattered body—a human equivalent of a Magic Eye poster.

I'd hold the autostereogram person to my face, eyes blurred, and when we slowly pulled away from one another, I could see the meaning in their patterns.

***

My face is covered in reddish freckles that start brown and turn into the color of chestnuts. They are almost everywhere: nose –cheeks forehead– ears–arms–legs–chest. But Robert had freckles in coiled compositions that I didn't share: russet dimples that pinpointed individual places that I'd explore with my fingertips and the tips of my pointed incisors. I would have liked to swallow up each auburn stain.

I wanted the same circles of peppery hail that curved with his facial expressions, the ones that would twist his emotions into precious astral planes. Seas of cosmos decorated a universe of feelings.

Each point of rust tasted like metal to my lunar mouth.

Maybe I wanted the particles of his melanin to live inside me, somewhere near my always-hungry stomach. They'd fall through my lips and down my throat, polka-dotting my epiglottis and coasting along my insides like that 7-Up game from my childhood. They'd collect in spiced arrangements in the slick film of my insides—my heart covered in spots—and at that moment we would be shared human freckles, absorbing sunlight despite grey days.

Building a Bouquet out of Baby's Breath Alone

Every woman I've passed today has been wearing perfume that's a scent from a hopscotch-block memory of my life: collections that are organized in lopsided chalk outlines, out-of-focus in their bygone lives. The commute from 11th street station to the 69th Street station is a time machine fashioned out of the limbic system—I travel through stretches of the past, driven by mood, memory, behavior, and emotion. The limbic system is primitive, found in the very first mammals.

We are all connected to the past.

I inhale bodies on the platform of the subway stop at 11th Street and am filled with the shape of these emotions that hold weight like water in sweating glasses—melting ice cubes that you try to pull the ragged last tastes of whiskey from.

There is a twisted curl of a woman standing on the yellow safety-bump-marked line next to me who smells like perfume from the Body Shop that I thought was so sexy when I was in my early twenties, when all the witches who I surrounded myself with smelled like sandalwood and also sort of like the receptionist from my high school. Before boarding the oncoming subway, the woman shakes out tresses like unfurling a flag, the scent of heavy yellow leaves billowing behind her: aromatic wood. I am a stern in the wake. As we enter the subway car, humidity pours over us. The heaviness of the clammy interior is impenetrable and uncomfortable like first kisses.

Some scientists believe that kissing developed from sniffing, shuffling close to a person to draw their scent into your body. First kisses: a primal behavior where we smell and taste our partner to decide if they're a match.

In the silver-bullet body of the train, next to me on the blue plastic seats, is a cool arm belonging to a dark-haired woman. She periodically brushes against my body. She is cloaked in the scent of off-brand Tommy Girl body glitter gel. It smells like the kind I used to buy at CVS to replicate the 7th-grade popular girls with their real designer perfume. I would coat my body with the gel, a slick reptilian skin smelling sour like rubbing alcohol and fermented flowers. Later I would scrub the specks off me, born anew every night—every flake a Daughter of Danaus. The popular girls with their swaying ponytails never liked me, and they certainly didn't like me in the way that I liked them and, by extension, all girls. The cool arm exits the train at 15th street, leaving the memories of grade school behind her.

As the subway sways past graffiti in forgotten tunnels—stops that no longer gather passengers—I meditate on moments from my youth where I could have been brave but wasn't. I re-create playground scenes with loose limbs dangled upside down on monkey bars, with hair follicles contracting into goose skin after flesh-to-flesh encounters. And how my best friend smelled like the Hawaiian Barbie my brother got me for Christmas a few years earlier, both of them—the friend and the doll—with so much long brown fig-colored hair in waves to the small of their backs. The week before that Christmas, I crept through the closet to find the gift, my short hair scratching my neck like a crumb brush. The doll came with a solid perfume balm, and it smelled like islands to which I have never been.

My best friend and I stopped talking in high school; she chose boyfriends and proffered cans of Pabst Blue Ribbon while I pretended that my emotions for her were merely platonic. She took the scent of Barbie balm with her. Young love is always hard.

High school was and is all longing, and it carried the fragrance of blueberries, and blueberries reduced, and blueberries reduced again: lip gloss from Bath & Body Works in glass cups that I painted over my mouth and then licked off. I gave myself all the kisses I wanted, held myself in solo embraces, walked my fingers up the staircase of my spine, ran hands over the curve of my puppy belly. Every day was an outfit, like a riddle that I never quite figured out—am still confused about in so many ways as an adult. Now I try to piece together the frenetic ardor of my teenage self, the jigsaw fragments of emotions that haunt me whenever I see a pretty woman on the train like why do baby's breath look so lonesome as they surround the crowned-head blossom of roses?

The train maintains its course to 69th Street with a fresh slew of well-dressed bodies creating volume in the sweating cars at the 30th Street stop. Coltishly-shaped men with square-framed glasses dart through the doors—30th Street station Clark Kents—followed by briefcases and the clatter of heels. An expensive fragrance permeates the world of the train car, and the scent belongs to the kind of women with haircuts that speak for them—dagger-sharp bob edges that ask, "Where are the twist-off bottles of rosé?" Haircuts and smells and jobs and relationships that I will never be able to break into. The old swinging ponytails have been cut into right angles. The woman wearing the designer fragrance is elegant, with clavicles that sing sonnets. She chooses to stand by the electronic doors and gaze in the moody detached way that only beautiful people can perfect.

On some days I fall in love with ten different women on the way to work.

Barreling forward, pitted tunnels and bridges make up the grey world of the subway. They create edges around the city linking the concrete and the green—two different biospheres circling the conurbation. Bodies replace one another on the seat next to me, a parade of sweet and fetid and flowery and feelings that don't yet have names but are as real to me as joy and sadness. In the swaying cradle of the car, my emotions are a flightless bird. With each revolving person, I am at once an ostrich and an ogre. A girl sits next to me, snapping bubblegum with the alien eyes of her sunglasses reflecting the faces of all the passengers. Her face is a canvas, and in the periphery, I see myself parched with the ache of hunger, unsure of what the craving is for.

The 69th Street terminal is the last stop. It smells like pizza that bubbles with life: boiling rolling seas of cheese. Banks of pretzels fog the end of the commute, and coffee brewing in the bodega screens the station. My mouth fills with warmth from pockets of saliva. The $27 in my pocket makes me feel like a millionaire even though there are holes in the bottoms of my shoes that have soaked up the end-of-winter sludge. As I walk through the station, I leave prints in my wake like the facial impression of a bloody sweating Christ—the soles of my shoes, Veronica. The tears leak through the soles; my face is dry.

The cloud of scent hangs above my head, and as I navigate through the swarm of bodies, memories continue to rain down on me. Brief almost-tastes of instances glimmer just out of reach. Phantoms of desire flow over my worn clothing—they shroud my holey shoes. How do you outrun longing? If I lost the pathway to smell, would I also lose the tender sting of sentimentality?

Even though everything itches with scent memories, I find comfort upon reaching the pizza place. Pizza for breakfast, like I dreamt when I was a kid. I buy the extra-large slice of pepperoni, knowing there is even enough for a big cup of soda to go with it. Inside the warmth of the shop, everything smells like the color orange. It darts a ray through the haze of past bodies.

I raise the triangle to my mouth over and over, the same action and taste and smell that brought me joy throughout the confusion of my childhood, teenage, and adult longings.

We're all connected to our own personal past.

In the solitude of my communion, I imagine building a bouquet made of baby's breath alone. Every bobbing filler flower comprised of sacrosanct bodies waiting to be worshipped, giving off their heady scent and filling people with wanting.

Desert Gardens

I fantasized about killing Allison. About how I would like to set up a pyre made from her own bones and roast the remaining pearly skin and use her tawny curls as kindling—slow torture to make up for times I was too unguarded to know better. She mirrored my behavior, aping my language and pilfering the protected parts of my small life. Allison became the best parts of me.

One day I had an existence. One day I had Allison.

We lived together by circumstance—sat on trash-picked, needle-pointed rugs and played at being bohemians. At night we would get drunk on shitty vodka and she would follow me to my room's private bathroom, trying to watch me while I peed even though I was pee shy. She would grab my hand and lead me to the bed, a silent imploration to heal twin lonesomeness.

In the grey mornings, Allison would mother me with apple cake and strong black coffee and argue that our friendship shouldn't be sullied with sex. Crumbs on my face, I eagerly concurred. All my friends had stopped talking to me—stopped coming to the apartment—since Allison centered herself in the apex of my world. She was everything I had.

But she still managed to sully me with sex—even when it wasn't with her.

***

Allison encouraged her drug-addicted friend, nameless in my memory, to fuck me—a shadowy figure that visited me during night terrors, black hair dipped over one luminous eye. Held me down with arms riddled in pockmarks while I was eyes-glazed drunk in a park: "You're more fun when you're fucked up." He was a daily visitor to the coffee shop she worked at— Allison's only other friend. The three of us together buried our faces in alcohol the first night I met him, until with nods and winks, the wight and I were left alone.

In the morning, I peeled the pink dress with the grass stains off of the shell of my body, sat in a tub with water as hot as it could get, and read a book I found on the sidewalk three weeks earlier: *Caddie Woodlawn*. It was a book I once read as a kid. In the bathtub, I imagined myself as a sunburnt child again. The next room over was Allison's room with the orange couch that she liked to coil up on. I could hear her listening to music. The hot water burned the soft folds of my insides.

Sometimes she would draw funny pictures of me, writing the word "tease" underneath cartoon-me. Allison and the ghost boy once presented an illustrated picture of me as an elf, my hair wild under a green pointy cap. My eyes looked sad in the picture.

Both would feed me sex and drinks, and then condemn me for it. "You shouldn't drink so much," Allison said as we downed gin and tonics on the floor of the living room, watching movies we had liked as children—only now enjoying them as detached child-adults. "I think you'd be really fun on coke," the ghost said, a few moments later. "Coke *is* really fun," Allison agreed, nodding. She pushed her long beautiful fingers through my hair; "We should all do it together someday."

Carbonation made drinks fluffier and grievances sorrowful, so I would drink from my cask until I would eventually float away while in their presence. The chatter of the duo was a staccato rhythm in the background of my brain's blackness. The three of us were a circle on the carpet, so alone individually while together.

"I feel really protective of you," she once said as we sat at opposite ends of a kitchen table like we were a mom and dad, our ghost son in the bathroom, probably shooting up. Maybe protection was the same as isolation when it came to weak-willed, wild-eyed girls like me.

In the mirror of my bathroom, I talked riotously about murdering Allison and how I could finally be free of her and the twins we'd become. An absence of humans to confide in, my phone packed with texts from an unfettered ghost (*if only you'd have just fucked me, I wouldn't have had to do smack last night*), I unburdened my darkest desires to the mirror-world me. "Hey, pretty bird! I made us dinner," Allison's voice trilled outside my door. I let my hand hang on the doorknob, forehead pressed against the barrier.

***

Allison moved to Texas. I didn't kill her. She decided to move in with a woman who had eyes like Southern Comfort, a musician who dined on raw vegetables at all hours. Strong. Allison was her lime juice.

Before Allison left, she came in my room and sat on the bed, hand in my hair; she told me, "When I get to Texas, I'm going to grow gardens in the desert."

The Pool, August 2002

We fell asleep in the sun, and when I woke up, I was so sunburned that, later that night, I got sick to my stomach. It was the summer that smelled like chlorine and cigarettes; we were staying at my parents' friends' house.

No one else we knew had a pool. Our fingers and toes became so pruned that they developed sores from too many hours in the water. "My eyes feel like they're going to bleed," you said, squinting from the chemicals; they looked greener than usual.

"1, 2, 3!" We would plunge under the water and shout a word; the other person had to guess the muffled sounds. On the third day, you made me wear a shirt while we swam because the reflection would make my blistering skin worse.

Despite the zinc, my nose began to peel, and we left two days later.

In the autumn we broke back into the house to try and re-create the whole thing, but we uncovered the pool and found dirty leaves and frozen water.

A Citadel Made of Human Bones

You stood at the base of the stairs holding out a pair of jeans, offering them to me. "You might fit into these. They're too small for me now." I took the denim from your callused freckled hand and looked at the digits—pink skin with dirty, long, calcium-rich fingernails. I thought about how all the parts of you—solid and dense, soft and stiff at the same time—were luminous. How every fragment of your body was stippled with fine russet hairs that I wanted to spend my entire life counting. How was that a glorious possibility? I pressed the jeans to my cheek. They were too small for me.

Later in bed, our bodies touched side by side. With every rise and fall from your exhalations, while we listened to the rain stick sound of hail on the roof, I thought about building monuments on you with my tongue and teeth, and I purred emotions on the nape of your neck with the bend of my nose. You pet my head and said, "You're a good girl."

I am a good girl.

Throughout the remainder of the month, I'd open my drawer and see the faded too-small-for-me-too jeans and think about how you wore them during previous pre-me years. I'd run my fingers over the grain of the fabric, wondering what had been rooted in the fibers—your history. I wanted to take your past in my mouth, chew on it and digest it and grow from it.

I yearned to burrow in the twill of your old clothes, become indistinguishable from the diagonal parallel ribs.

When you left, I started to drop pound after pound, and I wondered what parts of me I was losing with the weight. Did they carry memories? Meals we ate together. Long shadowed afternoons on a couch, dying on our phones. I'd grab the extra portions of my flesh and ask the meat to stay in its place, keeping you alive through corporeality. But my body never obeyed me. Instead, I put on the jeans and wore the recollections like a pelt. Stained with grease from some moment in your past that I'll never know, I hitched up the loose waistline from the belt loop—did you do that, too? I wore the jeans until my own history started to accumulate in the ribbing.

Two months later, in the clamor of your home hub, I went to pick up the debris of a life together, watched you cry, felt nothing while your face creased. My hips cocked like Billy the Kid, dipped at one side with the jeans slouching down, I was a snake slipping out of its skin. The scales of your pants wilting off my body exposed the fresh flesh underneath inch by inch. When you pulled me to you by the belt loops, I saw the friendly faces of each tiny hair that I had spent my time identifying.

We stacked our body parts one atop the other— made a citadel of human bones. You pulled me out of the jeans you gave me—an article of clothing you said you wore when you were at your "most fuckable." Well, what am I if I'm the one that wears them now?

I told myself that it was revenge sex, but who was I getting revenge on if I end up getting hurt, too? And by hurt, I mean that I am a good girl that feels everything intensely. But I didn't and don't know a word or feeling that means sad-but-relieved-at-the-same-time.

I am a good girl that left your house that day with your jeans, and my rubble, and the pebbles of your voice in my head—our shared sweat on my arms like a hide. And I couldn't wait to get home and mortar the past off my skin.

Emphatic Evenings

I drank wine out of a cup, bottle next to it. In the middle of the night, I woke up wanting cold pizza. Cold lemonade.

But realized that, while blacked out, I ate all the pizza. And drank all the lemonade.

And I didn't even have the sense to enjoy it while it was there.

Now my stomach hurts. My mouth is thick.

End

Acknowledgments

The following pieces have appeared in the following journals:

"Couches I knew in my 20s", "Emphatic Evenings", #*thesideshow* (*Five 2 One Magazine*)

"After you survive the fallout–shed", "Hypnotized with Motion", *Maudlin House*

"Cartographer", *Literary Orphans*

"Red Oxide of Iron", *Nottingham Review*

"Family of Four Lokos", "The Origin of Trees" *Vending Machine Press*

"Ocean Songs for the Nursery", "Pendulum Pastry" *Jellyfish Review*

"A Thicket. A Glen", *Hobart*

"Shrimp Backs", *Bedfellows Magazine*

"Cards on the floor in the shape of a T", *Slink Chunk Press*

"The practice of eating apples with glass teeth", *Easy Street Magazine*

"The shape of rain", *Five on the Fifth*

"The Binding Sequence", *New South Journal*

"Bison Called Buffalo", *Drunk Monkeys*

"Freckles", *SHARK REEF*

"Building a bouquet out of baby's breath alone", *Bending Genres*

"Desert Gardens", *Pigeonholes*

"The Pool, August 2002", *Mulberry Review*

"A Citadel of Human Bones", *Crab Fat Magazine*

www.ingramcontent.com/pod-product-compliance
Lightning Source LLC
Chambersburg PA
CBHW070354120726
47909CB00008B/2848